Seashells

TREASURES FROM THE NORTHEAST COAST

WRITTEN AND ILLUSTRATED BY

J. ROACH-EVANS

Published by
Islandport Press
P.O. Box 10
267 U.S. Route One, Suite B
Yarmouth, Maine 04096
books@islandportpress.com
www.islandportpress.com

ISBN: 1-978-1-934031-79-7
Library of Congress Control Number: 2012945242
Printed in the United States

For Katy, with love,

and special thanks to my father
for sharing his love
of the seashore with me

There is a special place
where the land
meets the sea.

This special place is
called the beach.

The beach is a magical place.
If you look down at your feet
where the ocean has left the sand,
there is no end
to the treasures you might find.

Along the sand
and in among the rocks,
there are marvelous seashells
of every kind.

Many of these shells were once
homes for animals called *mollusks.*
Mollusks are marine animals that have soft bodies.
They make unique shells to protect themselves.
There are many different kinds of shells
because there are many different kinds of mollusks.

Finding these shells is like going
for a treasure hunt on the beach.

Many of the shells you find
belong to either a class of mollusks, called *gastropods*,
that have one shell, or a class of mollusks, called *bivalves*,
that have two shells.

One of the most beautiful shells of all
belongs to a gastropod
called the *Northern Moon Snail.*
It makes one spiral shell—amazing!

Two cousins of the Northern Moon Snail
are the *Slipper Snail* and the *Tortoise-shell Limpet.*
They both make one shell.

Can you find the Slipper Snail's shell?
Slipper Snails are sometimes called Boat Snails.

Can you find the 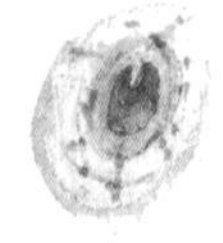 Tortoise-shell Limpet?

Both the Slipper Snail and the Tortoise-shell Limpet
like to hang tightly on to rocks (and sometimes each
other) so they are not washed away by the tide.

Have you seen
one of these?
It is the little door
of the Northern
Moon Snail. These doors
are called operculum
(Latin for "little lid").

Another mollusk
that creates a spiral shell
is the *Periwinkle*.

Periwinkles also hang on to rocks.
About one inch long, periwinkles
are smaller than Northern Moon Snails.

If you look on and
around large rocks at
the edge of the beach,
you are sure to see
many periwinkles.

Tip: You might have to lift up seaweed and look underneath.

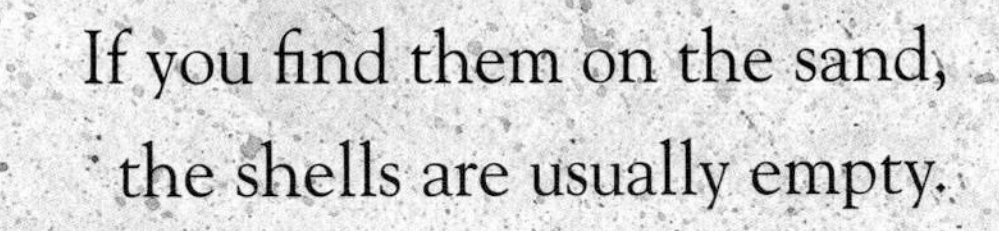

If you find them on the sand,
the shells are usually empty.

Keep looking. You might find one
with a snail still in it!

(p.s. Please don't keep it. It will die.)

If you are very lucky you may discover some of the largest mollusk shells of all, the whelks.

This is a *Knobbed Whelk*, named for the knobs on its shoulder.

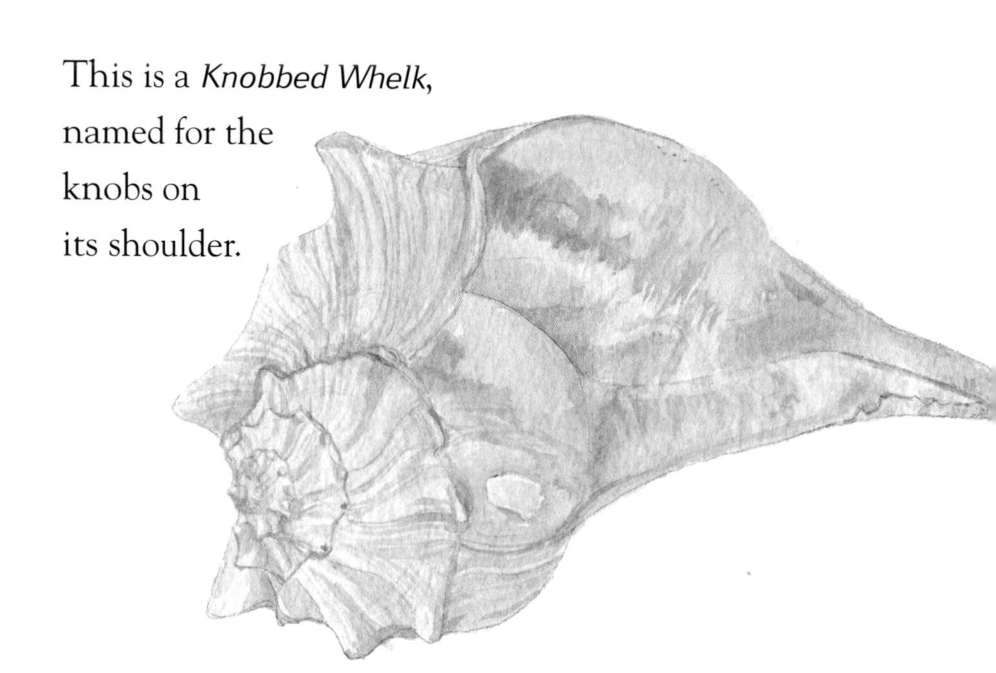

The *Channeled Whelk*
can grow to be seven inches long.

The shells of the clam family are more common.
They may be the first shells you find.

The *Surf Clam* belongs to the class of mollusks called the bivalves. They have two shells that are hinged together.

Look at the large shells of the Surf Clam.
See the lines on the shell?
They are called growth lines. They tell the age of the clam. Each line represents one year.

There are many different types of clam shells.

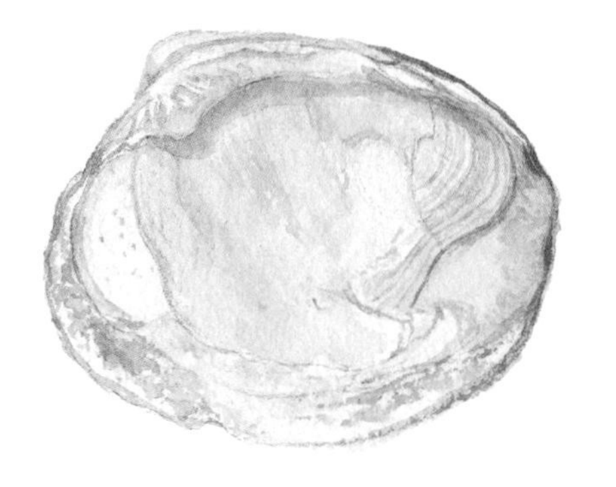

This beauty is a hard-shelled clam called the *Northern Quahog* *(pronounced "ko-hog").*

This is a *Ribbed Pod*, also called an *Atlantic Razor Clam.*

Soft-shelled Clams are common, but the shells break easily.

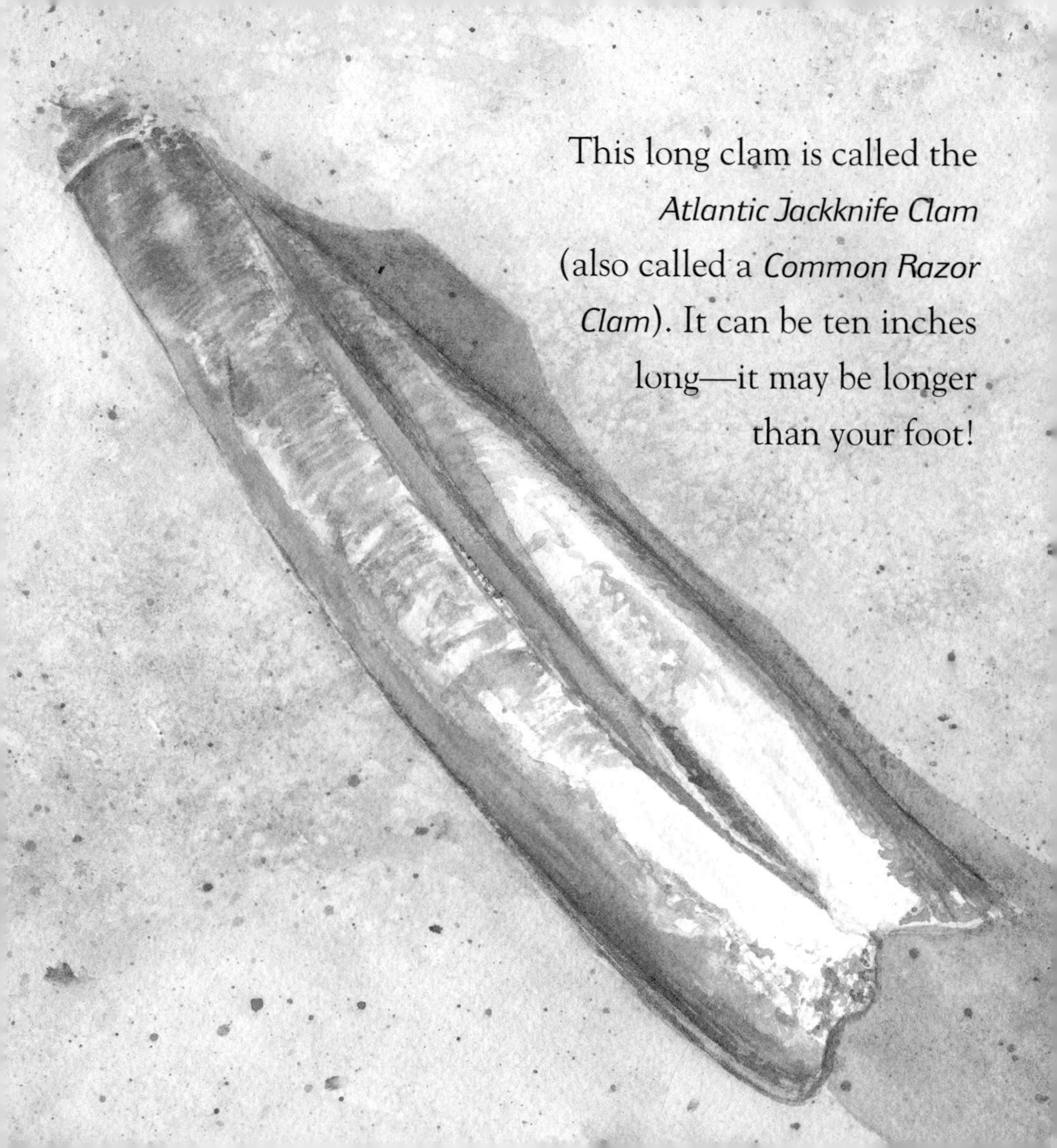

This long clam is called the *Atlantic Jackknife Clam* (also called a *Common Razor Clam*). It can be ten inches long—it may be longer than your foot!

One of the smaller bivalves is the little *Jingle Shell.* These are called Jingle Shells because of the sound they make when they touch each other.

Try holding them in your hand or in a cup and shake them to hear them jingle. You can string them on a cord and hang them in the wind.

They are also called toe nails. I think you can see why!

Scallops also have two shells.
Scallops are very common on
Cape Cod's beaches in Massachusetts.
They have beautiful,
neatly patterned shells.

The Jingle Shells and Scallops come in all colors. See how many you can find.

Common Blue Mussels are a bit larger
and longer than Scallops.
They are often found clinging to rocks under water.
Sometimes they get washed up on shore.

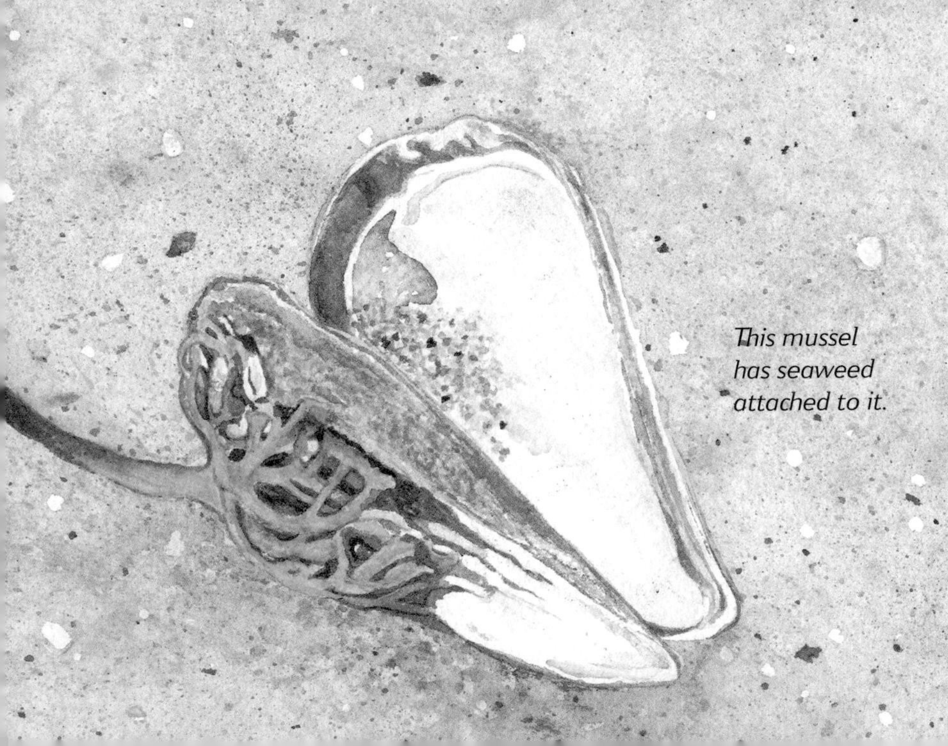

This mussel has seaweed attached to it.

These are the craggy, rough shells
of the *Oyster.*
Inside the shells,
it is smooth and shiny.

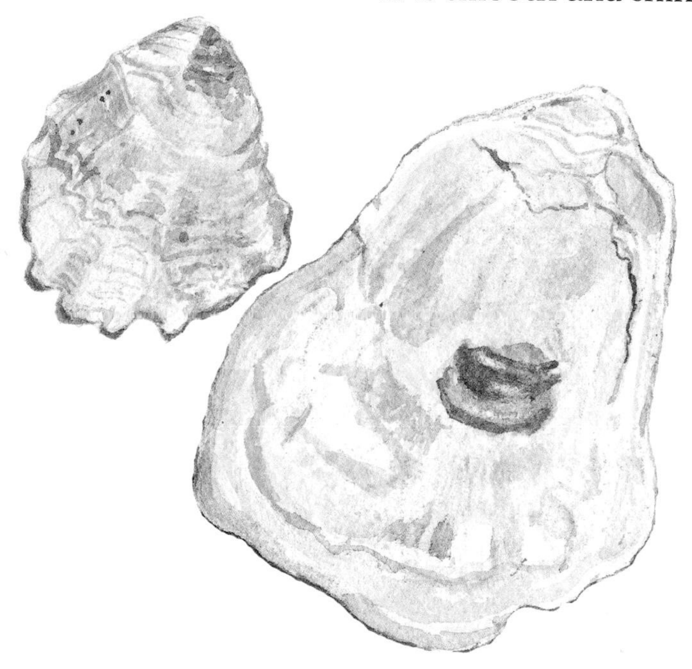

Not all the shells you find
on the beach are from mollusks.
You may find the shell
of a *Sand Dollar.*

It is rare to find a
whole one like this.
The chalky shell is delicate
and breaks very easily,
so be very careful if you find one.

*More often,
you find broken
bits like these.*

*The sand dollar
is closely related to
the sea urchin.*

*This is shown larger
than actual size.
They are usually about
three inches across.*

You might even find a fish bone
—beautiful.

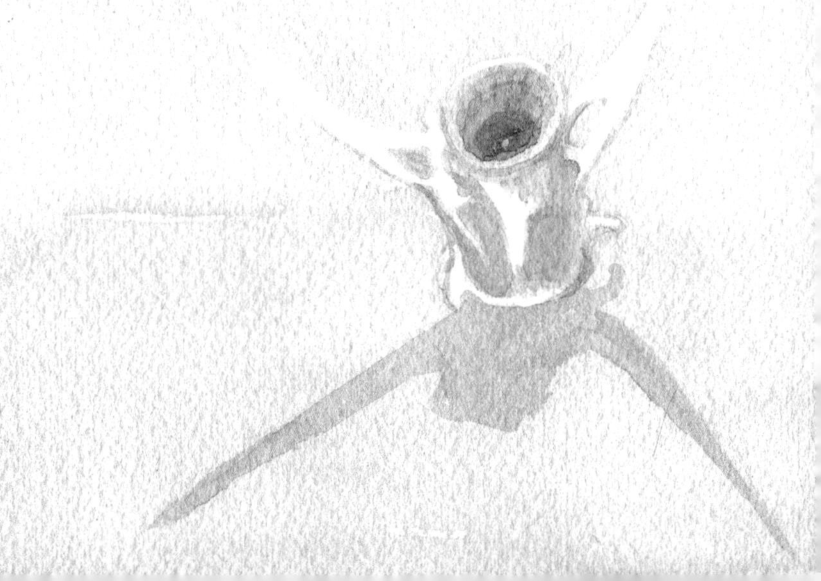

Walk slowly and look closely,
and you're sure to find something
remarkable, your own treasure
from the beach.

GASTROPODS

(one shell)

Periwinkle snails

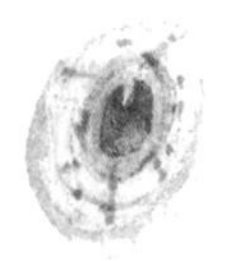

Tortoise-shell Limpet

Northern Moon Snail

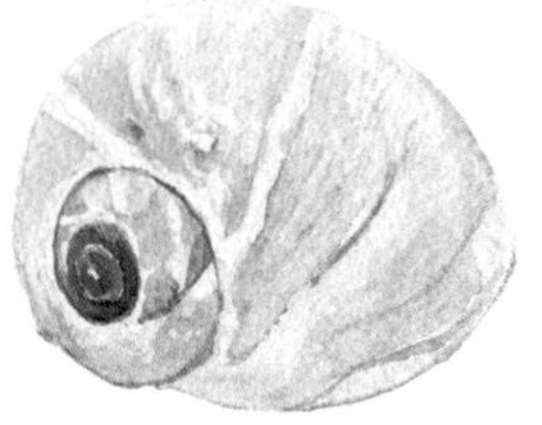

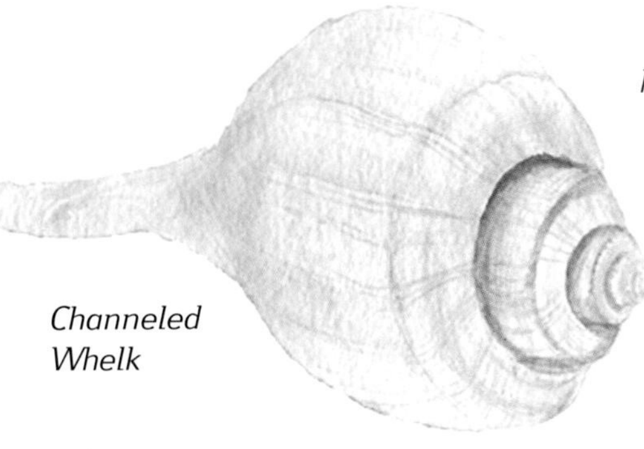

Channeled Whelk

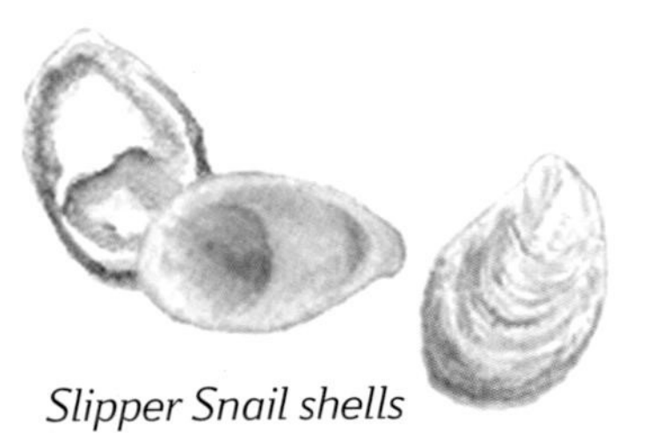

Slipper Snail shells

Knobbed Whelk

BIVALVES

(two shells)

Jingle shells

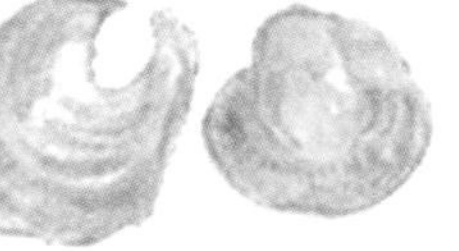

Soft-shelled clam

Oyster shells

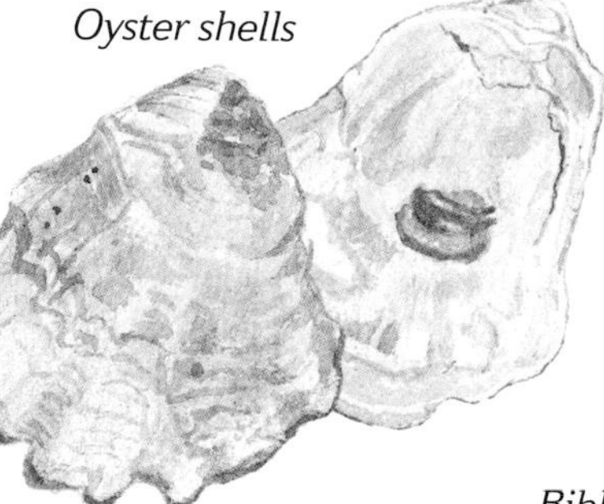

Hard shell clam or Quahog

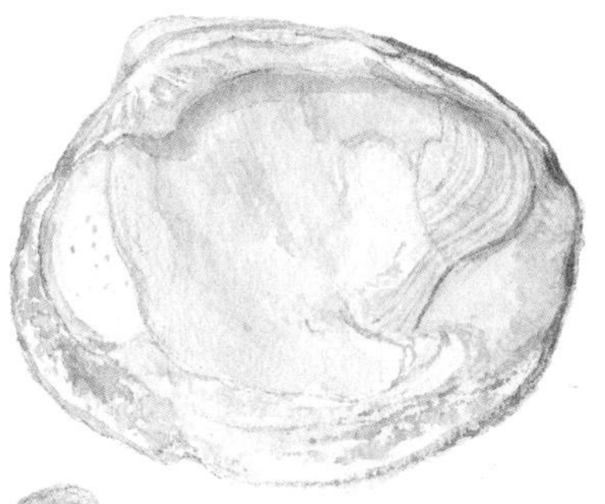

Ribbed Pod

Mussel shell

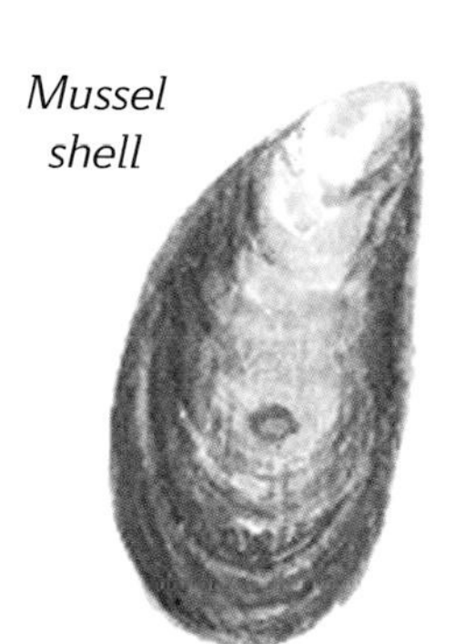

Scallop shell

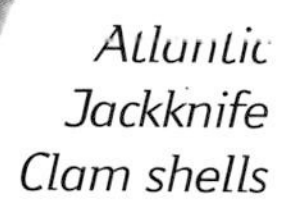

Atlantic Jackknife Clam shells

ABOUT THE AUTHOR

Joanne Roach-Evans wrote and illustrated her first children's book at age nine and decided that she would grow up to be a children's book author and illustrator. She pursued her passion for art at the School of the Worcester Art Museum and her love of writing at Worcester State University where she received a BFA in English and a Masters in Education. She currently teaches art and graphic design. As a curious naturalist, she draws inspiration from the natural world and expresses it in her writing and painting. When she's not teaching, writing, or painting, she can be found beachcombing along New England's shores. She lives in central Massachusetts with her husband, two sons, and a garden full of birds.

AUTHOR'S NOTE *It took me many years to find all the shells in this book. So take your time, enjoy the hunt, and don't expect to find everything in one day, one week, or even one year!*

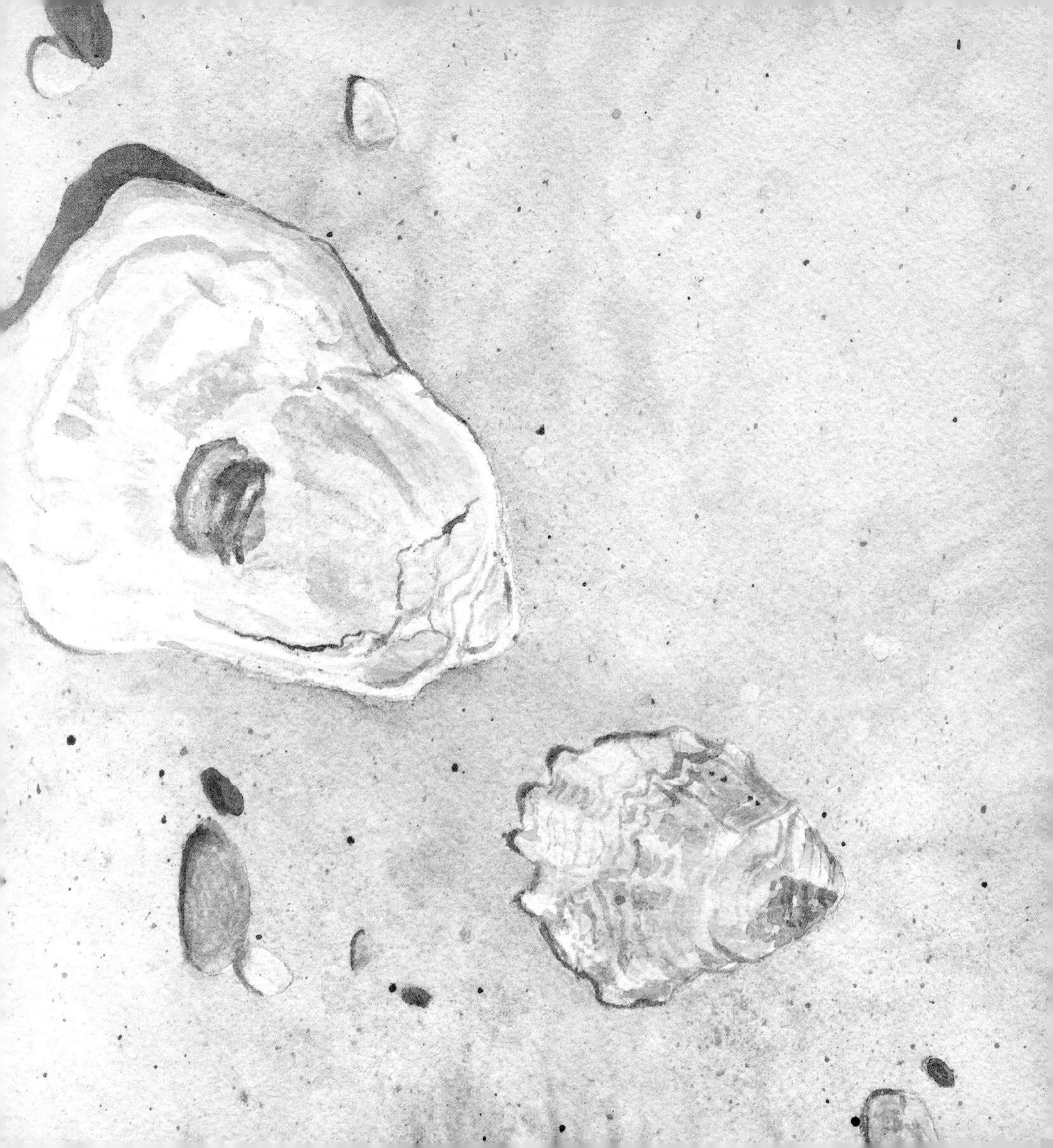

Maine
New
Hampshire
Massachusetts
Connecticut
RI
New
Jersey
NY